ISN'T THAT THE MAN WHO....

OVERCOMING THE LABELS THAT HAVE BEEN PLACED ON US

DALLAS STRINGER

BookVenture Publishing LLC
1000 Country Lane Ste 300
Ishpeming MI 49849
www.bookventure.com
Hotline: 1(877) 276-9751
Fax: 1(877) 864-1686

Ordering Information:
Quantity sales. Special discounts are available on quantity purchases by corporations, associations, and others. For details, contact the publisher at the address above.

Printed in the United States of America.

ISBN-13:	Softcover	978-1-64348-534-2
	Pdf	978-1-64348-535-0
	ePub	978-1-64348-536-9
	Kindle	978-1-64348-537-7

Rev. date: 11/03/2018

CONTENTS

ACKNOWLEDGMENT

There are so many I would like to thank for helping make this dream a reality. Our Father in Heaven deserves all credit and glory, for without Him we would not be. And, because of Him, I was blessed with a support system who believed in me and this project.

Shelby Boyd, thank you for helping put my thoughts into a readable content. You did a great job. Marty and Krissy Field, thank you for your help with editing and other behind the scenes work. I'm thankful for your friendship. Jack McCarty, thank you for your encouragement to write this book. Kevin Oakley and Micah Meurer, you two men of God have been my closest friends for years. Your inspiration and guidance is invaluable. Dr. Randy Davis, thank you for your mentorship in ministry. You are truly my "father in the faith" and I will never be able to thank you enough.

Calvary Baptist Church and Eastmont Baptist Church, being able to be your Pastor at specific moments in time was and is a calling I never deserved and greatly underperformed, but you have loved me through my inadequacies. Thank you!

To my mother-in-law, Diane, thank you so much for the final edit. You are great, and that work was helpful to many. Mom, I love and adore you. To my wife and kids, you will never understand how deeply I love you guys. The fact that we are a family means everything to me. I love you and and I am eternally grateful for you.

Dallas Stringer

SAUL, THE MAN WHO...

I had a reputation when I was young. Living in a small town in rural Texas, word gets around. When I was growing up, I earned all kinds of labels I had to live down later in my life.

I can remember a time in the fourth grade when the teacher was calling roll. It was the very first day of class. When she got to my name she paused, then she stood up and walked around the room to where I was. I'll never forget the look in her eyes when she found me.

I went home and told my dad about the experience.

"Yeah, she hated me in school," he responded flatly.

"What?"

"Yeah, she didn't like your mom in school either."

"Man, this isn't fair!" I cried in answer. I hadn't even done anything yet and I was already being labeled. I was going to do something. It was going to happen. But I already had a reputation to live down on day one.

I remember asking a girl out once, and her parents said no. "I know who your father is. I don't think we want her to go out with you."

I wasn't a bad kid – I wasn't terrible – but that was the reputation I had because of who my parents were.

I had my own reputation to deal with too. Who I was in life, how I acted, responded to things, and the attitude I had wasn't always positive. I got in trouble all the time. I was given swats every year from kindergarten through my senior year of high school.

My senior year I thought that I had made it through without discipline. I had a new teacher, it was almost the end of the year, and "Man!" I thought, "This was it." I was going to get through the year without a single swat.

My teacher was a big, tall guy, who had played basketball in college. My buddy and I were messing around in class and he told us, "Quit it or I'll have to send you to the office for tomfoolery."

"I've never met Tom Foolery. Why do I have to go to the office for Tom Foolery?" I "innocently" asked.

"Dallas," he warned, "I'm not playing around. You need to cut it out."

Suffice it to say, I didn't cut it out.

"Congratulations, boys," he said. "You get to be the first people I have to give swats to."

We went in to the principal's office, I'll never forget this, and he asked, "Who wants to go first?"

Which, by the way, you always want to volunteer to go first because that's just the warm up. So, I bent over my principal's desk and looked back at my teacher. He stood about six-foot-nine, and I watched as he stretched his arm back.

And back.

And back.

Until BAM.

Tears filled my eyes. It had been a long time since swats had made me cry. As I walked out of the office, my buddy's eyes grew wide at the sight of my tears. I could see the worry all over his face. I gingerly took my seat as he went in to the principal's office. The door shut behind him. I waited then heard his swat through the door. I was still hurting from mine. The door opened and the principal was laying over the top of his desk, just laughing.

Together my buddy and I walked out the door and the teacher said, "Y'all get back to class. I need to talk to the principal for a minute."

As we went back to class, my buddy was crying. I mean, we were seniors in high school and he was just sobbing.

"Are you gonna be okay?" I asked.

"Did he spin around when he hit you?"

Apparently, our teacher had stretched back, just like with me, but when his arm was extended as far as it would go, he turned on his heels and spun on the spot, building momentum before making contact.

That teacher is now a missionary in the Philippines. I found him on social media and messaged him. "Mr. Hill, it's so good to see you."

His response was, "Remember that time I gave you swats?"

Yes, I did.

Those are the things you can't live down. The idea of who we used to be seems to follow us into our future lives. It labels us forever.

If you begin looking through the Bible you see people defined by who they once were. Labeled forever. You see Rahab, the prostitute, who will always be Rahab, the prostitute, no matter the great things she did for the Lord. Even in Hebrews, in "the hall of faith," you find her with that label.

But why? You don't see Abraham listed as "the man who told everyone his wife was his sister." You do not see Noah as "the one who got drunk." Moses isn't "the one who struck the rock." However, certain people are labeled by who they once were.

Our church held services in a large tent for a couple of weeks one summer. I was preaching out of Acts and this passage spoke to me that day.

Immediately he began proclaiming Jesus in the synagogues: "He is the Son of God." But all who heard him were astounded and said, "Isn't this the man who..."
Acts 9:20-21a (HCSB)

Saul is proclaiming the gospel and the only thing the people can think about is who Saul used to be. They cannot get past "the man who..." and they even start listing all of the things he had done. Everything the people listed was true.

He did persecute the church.

He did try to kill the Christians.

He did try to destroy the movement of Christ.

The first time we see Saul is while men are getting ready to execute Stephen. Saul stood by watching as these men, whose cloaks he held, stoned Stephen to death. He was so important to the anti-Christian reaction, that the very first image we see of him is holding the cloaks of the men who executed the first Christian martyr. He was obsessed with destroying the church. He was an angry man, determined to stop the spreading of what was referred to as "the Way." All of the things the disciples were questioning when they asked "Isn't that the man who…" were true. It was who Saul was.

In Acts 9, starting in verse 1, before our story starts, it says that

Meanwhile, Saul was still breathing threats
and murder against the disciples of the Lord. He
went to the high priest and requested letters from
him to the synagogues in Damascus,
so that if he found any men or women who
belonged to the Way,
he might bring them as prisoners to Jerusalem.
Acts 9:1-2 HCSB

It was Saul's initiative that drove him. His desire was to stop any movement of Christ. Hatred spewed from his mouth and in Acts 26 he describes himself as "greatly enraged" toward the followers in Christ. He imprisoned many, voted for their execution, and even chased them down when they ran away. His one desire was to stop the movement of Christ.

I watched a lot of football when I was a kid. I had a video called *Thunder and Destruction: The Best of Sports Illustrated Hard Hits.* I remember watching this and seeing that there is a certain thing physics teaches us. It shows that if two men are running at each other full-force, and one is bigger, more powerful, stronger, and has the right leverage at the right time, that one will bull over the other man every time. When Saul decided to take on Jesus Christ, he messed with the wrong One. He decided he was big enough, smart enough, tough enough, and educated enough. Saul was described in history as bow-legged with a hooked nose. It is the same description usually given to Hercules. He was probably stout and strong. He was certainly educated and intelligent. But he tried to tackle the wrong God.

We know from his letters that Saul was traveling to Damascus to persecute the Christians when the Lord showed Himself. Saul states:

> *I was traveling and near Damascus, about noon an intense light from heaven suddenly flashed around me. I fell to the ground and heard a voice saying to me, "Saul, Saul, why are you persecuting Me?" I answered, "Who are You, Lord?"*
>
> **Acts 22:6-8a HCSB**

This is such a key verse. "Who are you, Lord?"

When I was a kid I used to wrestle around with my uncles. I was a wrestler all through school, but they were big guys. We would wrestle around and I thought I was pretty tough. I would be doing really well and then they would cheat. They would grab my toes and start twisting them. They would squeeze the inside of my thigh and that would be it. Game over. Every time they would get me they would yell "Say 'uncle!' Say 'uncle!'" I would fight it and fight it. I did not want to give in, but eventually the pain would get to me. I would realize there was nothing I could do to escape the grip they had on me. All I could do was submit and say "uncle!" I even had one uncle that would make me tell everyone that he was the best uncle I had, and that I loved him so much, and.... I couldn't even remember what he was telling me to say because it hurt so much, but I had to repeat it as he held me in his grip. He was in complete control.

Saul was walking on the road toward Damascus filled with anger and hatred. He was determined to destroy the church. Jesus appeared and shut him down. Saul fell to the ground and heard "Saul, Saul, why are you persecuting Me?" Saul realized he was in total submission. There was nothing he could possibly do. There was no way to escape and no way to get out. He cried out, "Who are you, Lord?" It's as if he is yelling "Who are you, Lord? Show yourself to me! I can't do this! I can't get up and I can't get out of this! There is nothing I can do to get away from this! Who are you? I am in total submission to you! You have my attention!"

How many times has God had to bring you to your knees to get your attention? How many times has he had to humble you to the very place where you couldn't move just to get you to focus on Him and say "Here I am! What is it you want from me? Tell me what it is you want because I will do anything." How often does He have to break us down to get us to listen?

The word Saul addresses Jesus with is not a word we use very often. We do not go to work and say to our boss, "Yes, my lord, whatever you tell me." I did not say, "Yes, my lord" when my wife woke me up to ask me to go feed our son. It does not work that way. There is only one Lord. At that moment in time, on the road to Damascus, Saul was in total submission to Him. The Lord had to break him down to nothing. Suddenly, Saul's intelligence, strength, power, agendas, and the letters giving him permission to arrest Christians did not matter. Not one thing in his life mattered at that moment except for the fact that the Lord Jesus Christ was trying to speak to him. Saul in his brokenness, absolutely destroyed, and in total submission cried out, "Who are you, Lord?"

"'I am Jesus the Nazarene, the One you are persecuting!'"... "And the Lord told me, 'Get up and go into Damascus, and there you will be told about everything that is assigned for you to do.'"

Acts 22:8b,10b HCSB

It does not matter what pew you sit in at church, it does not matter how long you are a member of a church, it does not even matter what church body you want to go to – all that matters is your relationship with Jesus Christ, identifying and being in total submission to Him. That is what matters.

Jesus told Saul to "get up and go." Do you then see Saul in his brokenness, after falling on his face and crying out to His Lord, saying, "No! I don't want to go! I'm not going to!" When you are broken down to the point that Saul had been, and God says, "Get up and go," you get up and go. When God humbles you like He humbled Saul, you listen. Saul, in his brokenness, got up and went.

Jesus was also preparing Ananias to go out and speak to Saul. Ananias, who is totally faithful and devoted to the Lord, hears the Lord's instructions to go and meet a man "from Tarsus named Saul" and to heal him. Ananias immediately switches from obedient to leery as he explains to God all of the things he has heard about this man named Saul. Imagine the backpedaling that happened inside of that conversation:

"Ananias!"

"Here I am, Lord!"

"I want you to go talk to Saul."

"I'm sorry, what was that? I'm getting a lot of static on my end. Are you going through a tunnel?"

The Lord tells Ananias again to go find Saul, and he finally obeys. When he found him, Ananias laid his hands on him and called him "Brother Saul." In that moment after crying out to the Lord, Saul came into complete submission to Him, and he became a part of the brotherhood of Jesus Christ.

I have been asked why I call myself "Brother Dallas" instead of "Priest." I want to be recognized as part of the brotherhood of Christ. I'd much rather be called brother than any other title you could give me. My chosen label is Brother. I want to be part of that family!

So Ananias left and entered the house. Then he placed his hands on him and said, "Brother Saul, the Lord Jesus, who appeared to you on the road you were traveling, has sent me so that you can regain your sight and be filled with the Holy Spirit." At once something like scales fell from his eyes, and he regained his sight. Then he got up and was baptized. And after taking some food, he regained his strength. Saul was with the disciples in Damascus for some days. Immediately he began proclaiming Jesus in the synagogues: "He is the Son of God."

Acts 9:17-20 HCSB

Immediately Saul went and began preaching and proclaiming Jesus in the synagogues. "He is the Son of God." Imagine! The last time he had been in the synagogue it was to get orders to persecute Christians. *Immediately* Saul was back in the synagogues, where everyone knew who he was and what he'd been doing, yet now he was proclaiming Jesus as the Messiah. Everyone stopped, looked at him, and began questioning, "Isn't that the man who…?"

Isn't that the man who persecuted, killed, and tried to destroy the Christian church? It is true. Saul, now Paul, says it over and over again that it *is* who he was and it *is* what he did. It is his story, his testimony. He leaves Damascus and goes to Jerusalem and his reputation is such that the disciples would not associate with him. They were all afraid of him!

I have preached in different countries, almost every major city in Texas, and in various areas all over the United States, but I have never once been invited to speak at my home church where I was saved and baptized. Why? Because my past precedes me. The truth is everything they want to say about me is probably true. I was a jerk. I was disobedient, I even got swats at boys' camp. I got in trouble, I snuck out, and I did it all over and over again. My past precedes me, and it is true.

It can take a while to live down who you used to be. People struggle so much with this. "I'm not that person anymore!" "I'm not having an affair! I'm not that person!" "I'm not that guy who takes drugs anymore!" But it *is* who you once were. It might take some time to live down who you once were, but stand up and be who God wants you to be today.

If I sit here and I cry and whine because I do not get to go to my old church and preach, it is not going to accomplish anything. But I can stand up and be who God wants me to be today. If the day comes and they call me back to go preach, even if it takes my whole life to live down who I was, I will go and I will share the Gospel, and I will rejoice with them.

We need to overcome in our lives. We need to let go of who we were. We need to stop worrying about who we used to be. We need to start moving forward with our lives, stop living in the past, and stop being concerned about who people think we are or what they have labeled us. Maybe in our own minds we can't let go of what we remember of our past. Maybe letting go of who we used to be seems impossible. Do not hold onto it!

It is time to overcome, and that starts with listening and submitting to the Lord. Step one is falling down in total submission and telling Him you are totally His. There are true believers out there who believe the truth of the Gospel and claim Jesus Christ as their savior but have never fully submitted to His lordship. Have you ever told the Lord, "I give everything to you?" The first step in letting go of who we used to be, in overcoming our past, is submitting to the Lord.

The second step in letting go of our past is confessing who you were, but forgetting what was behind you. Paul talked about it.

"But one thing I do: Forgetting what is behind and reaching forward to what is ahead."
Philippians 3:13b HCSB

Another thing you will see is Paul, over and over again, talking about his past. Paul continuously shared his testimony of who he used to be. How can he let go of his past while doing that? How can he move forward while constantly focusing on and sharing his testimony? Can anyone change the past?

If this book was published with a glaring typo and five copies with this mistake sold, could I change that? I could sit here and say, "If I had done this, or I had changed that, this never would have happened." But could I go back and correct the mistake? No, I can't. All I can do is move forward to what is ahead and live with the consequences. The person you were and the consequences of who you used to be is something you might still have to deal with.

People have approached me several times, telling me that the police are profiling them. "They're constantly after me! It's profiling!" But many of those people would not be being profiled today, if they hadn't committed crimes in the past. The police are profiling them because of who they used to be.

Stand up now and be the person you are today. Prove to the world you are not the same person you used to be. Forget who you were and press forward to be who God wants you to be today.

The third step is an important one. It may not be as important as submitting to the Lord. It may not be as important as pressing forward to who we are called to be, but it is important.

When he arrived in Jerusalem, he tried to associate with the disciples, but they were all afraid of him, since they did not believe he was a disciple. Barnabas, however, took him and brought him to the apostles and explained to them how Saul had seen the Lord on the road and that He had talked to him, and how in Damascus he had spoken boldly in the name of Jesus. Saul was coming and going with them in Jerusalem, speaking boldly in the name of the Lord.

Acts 9:26-28 HCSB

The third step in overcoming who you used to be is standing with people who can vouch for you. Stand next to someone who can say, "Yeah, that's who he used to be but not anymore!" Remember when Ananias went up and confronted Saul? He called him "Brother Saul." The idea is that he stood with Saul and put his arm around him and held him up. He believed in him and encouraged him. Do you know what often happens in the church today? Someone does something wrong and hurts another's feelings, and suddenly we are dead to each other. People leave church angry and upset. They never talk to each other again. We are not going forward with the Gospel of Christ. We are dividing it.

We also need to own up to our mistakes. We have to stand up and say, "I don't want to be that person anymore!" And we need someone to come alongside us and put their arm around us and stand with us.

When I was in college I could not figure out what I wanted to do with the rest of my life. I tried everything. I was going to study environmental science. I thought about theater and speech. I even considered education for awhile. Every time I tried something I failed. I just wasn't passionate about any of it. I remember sitting at a local restaurant with my dad in Amarillo when I told him, "I'm going to sign up for the fire academy. I'm going to be a firefighter." He started laughing.

"What are you laughing about? It's a noble profession!" I argued.

"No son, it's not that. Being a firefighter is a great thing. It's just that you were called to the ministry and everyone can see it but you. You are never going to be happy until you totally submit to the Lord."

In that moment it was like a key turned and everything inside of me flooded out in a rush of tears. I wept like a baby because I knew that I needed to submit everything to the Lord.

I'm not perfect. I fail over and over again, but He stands me up, and I submit to Him again. He guides me again. And again. And again.

The greatest moment of my life outside of receiving Jesus Christ as my Lord was when I submitted fully to Him. The Bible shows me that every knee will bow. I can look at the story of Saul and I can see how God humbled him and brought him to his knees. I can look in the Bible and see story after story of when God humbled people to get their attention. I am afraid that God will soon have to humble our country before we will turn to Him. We need to submit to Him long before that has to happen. We need to submit to Him and call Him Lord. We need to say, "I'm not going to look backwards! I'm going to look forward and press on!" We need people to stand up next to us and come around us to support us and hold us accountable.

If you are struggling with letting go of your past, you need to fall on your face and submit to the Lord. You need to hand everything over to Him and move forward. Find people who can stand next to you, vouch for you, and encourage you. If you have never submitted to Jesus Christ as Savior, you have to start there. You can live your life as who you used to be, or you can stand up and overcome. Let everyone say, "Isn't that the man who?" We can stand up together and show them who you are today.

SIMON THE LEPER

We all have a desire to be loved. If you don't believe me, just look at the Valentine's Day market! One night my daughter Ella, the youngest girl in my family, came running up the stairs. It was late and she was crying which could only mean one thing: bedtime.

"Ella, what's wrong? Aren't you spending the night with your brother or one of your sisters?"

"No!" she cried out between tears, "None of them will have me!"

To her this was a big deal. Even at a young age, she was showing her need to feel loved. There are adults in the world who feel the exact same way. They feel dejected, alone, and broken. They cry inside, feeling like nobody loves them, afraid no one will have them.

Before we talk about Simon the Leper, we first need to take a look at the book of Leviticus. Everyone's favorite book, right? In Leviticus 13 we find an entire section on how the Israelites were instructed to handle leprous people.

The person afflicted with an infectious skin disease is to have his clothes torn and his hair hanging loose, and he must cover his mouth and cry out, "Unclean, unclean!" He will remain unclean as long as he has the infection; he is unclean. He must live alone in a place outside the camp.

Leviticus 13:45-46 HCSB

This is only part of what had to happen if someone was found to have a skin disease. They were cast out, they had to cry out to everyone that they were unclean, and they even had to change the appearance of their hair and clothes. They were completely separated from the rest of their people.

If the priest declared someone clean, that person still had even more to go through to be able to come back into society. They had to shave all of the hair off of their head and body, stand outside of their tent, and make sure everyone knew they were now clean.

If the skin disease never went away and the person remained unclean, they were cast out, never to touch another human being again. They were absolutely isolated and alone.

Leprosy was a serious skin disease. They used to do experiments on people in the leper colonies. They would take objects that were important to the lepers who lived there and throw them in the fire. Then they would watch as the leper, whose skin was rotting away, would reach into the fire without pain to rescue their object.

How many times do you think they looked outside of their lonely tents toward their old homes and cried out, "No one will have me. I am alone! Nobody loves me."? How many times do you think they looked out for comfort and found none?

Once, I had these spots that started appearing on my skin that kept getting bigger. I had one place on my leg that was turning very red. It also itched terribly. I noticed that this particular spot started to wrap around my leg and I was getting no relief. I finally went to the doctor and asked him what was going on.

"It's psoriasis," he shrugged.

"What's that?"

"Oh, it's a form of leprosy."

All I could think was, "Oh great! Now I'm going to have to walk around town yelling 'I'm unclean! I'm unclean!'" Things are going to get awkward when someone tries to shake my hand at church. "I'm unclean! Stay away!"

I can't even imagine that kind of life.

We can all agree that Jesus led a perfect life. The Bible says that He was tempted in the same ways we are, but that He did not sin. If God's law called for Him to do something, He did it. If the law dictated He not do something, He didn't do it. He never violated God's law.

We can read in Leviticus that no one could be around someone with a serious skin disease yet here we see Jesus sitting in the house of Simon who was identified as one who had that very affliction.

While Jesus was in Bethany at the house of
Simon, a man who had a serious skin disease,
Matthew 26:6 HCSB

We can take away two very important things from this short verse. First, if Jesus never sinned then we know Simon must have been healed for Jesus to have been able to be near him. Jesus must have healed Simon of his skin disease! We know He has done it before. In the eighth chapter of Matthew, he healed another, unnamed leper. In order for Jesus to have been visiting Simon's house we know that Simon was healed.

The second thing we see is that *this* healing was just as miraculous as any other Jesus had performed. We do not need to have all of the details to come to that conclusion. Skin diseases were not that uncommon at this time. Knowing that and knowing that Simon was identified by his disease tells us that his outbreak had to have been a bad one.

"Simon? Simon who?"

"Oh, you know, the one with the skin disease."

"Oh, that guy. Yeah, I know that guy."

Once when we were in Israel, we had the opportunity to go eat at a first century dinner table. We had to sit down on the ground and lean on pillows. They would hand us a bowl full of food and some bread as we reclined on the floor. We were to take the bread and dip it in the bowl before passing the bowl to the next guy. So, I'm lying there watching the bowl get passed around. It gets to me and I cannot help myself. "Pass." Some of those people probably pick their nose! I do not want to share my food with them!

So, imagine you're sitting at the table with a man who is known as having a serious skin disease. He could easily reach his bread into the bowl to dip food out and instead leave a finger behind. I know. Gross. But that's exactly what could have happened here in Simon's house. He had been unclean. He had to be separated from society by his looks, by his location, and by his own declaration of "I'm unclean! I'm unclean!"

Then one day, an unassuming man walks up to him and heals him. His skin clears up. The open wounds close, and he is healed. He is clean. Remember the way everybody identified him as the man with the skin disease? Now instead of Simon the leper he has become Simon who used to have a skin disease.

Simon-who-used-to-have-a-skin-disease has Jesus the Messiah in his home. He has been healed and is back in his home. That is not where the story ends for him though. Through the next several verses, the focus changes to a woman who comes into the house, bringing with her an alabaster jar of very expensive perfumed oil. To the disciples' dismay she pours this oil on Jesus' head. In John chapter 12, we even see her bend down and pour some on His feet. She then wipes His feet clean with her own hair.

When the disciples saw it, they were indignant. "Why this waste?" they asked. "This might have been sold for a great deal and given to the poor."
Matthew 26:8-9 HCSB

Jesus calls what she has done "noble" and goes on to tell the disciples that:

...wherever the gospel is proclaimed in the whole world, what this woman has done will also be told in memory of her.
Matthew 26:13 HCSB

Even now we are telling the story about the woman who humbled herself to anoint Jesus with the oil and washed His feet with her hair.

And every time the story is told, it will begin with "...Jesus was in Bethany at the house of Simon, a man who had a serious skin disease."

I would like to share with you a testimony of a dear friend who very much felt the same way Simon the Leper did.

Rogelio "Mutt" Villarreal

My name is Rogelio. Once I was called Roger. Now I go by Mutt. My mom and dad for whatever reason decided not to raise me and instead gave me to my grandmother. She did the best she could with me, this wild kid, and I loved her. She died when I was eleven years old. I wasn't sure where I was going to live or who was going to take care of me. I bounced around from house to house. I took on a lot of responsibility for myself – I even had a utility bill in my own name at eleven. I went to my mom to ask her to take me in. She told me that if she was going to take care of me, she'd need to see about getting child support. I was confused. Child support? My dad is right there in the house with her!

That's when she told me he wasn't actually my father.

Years went by and soon I was twenty years old and married to my first wife. Drugs had a hold on me; different choices had led me to where I was then. I was hanging out and playing pool with my father when my first wife, completely out of the blue, said, "Tell us the truth. Roger's mom isn't really his mom, is she?"

"How did you know?" my father asked.

A few months later I sat down with my mom and she began telling me my story. The story of where I came from.

She told me that there were some extreme circumstances that she had to leave Texas and move to Oklahoma with her cousin who got her a job on a farm even though she was pregnant. I think they took pity on her since they were also pregnant with their first child. She shared a farm house with a welder and his wife. They became very close friends, and she trusted them so much that once she had me, she left me with them to go get my other brother in Mexico a couple weeks after she had me. While my mom was gone to Mexico, the farmer's wife had a miscarriage. They buried the baby and when my mother came back, the welder and his wife took her to the grave and told her, "This is where your baby died. Your baby is dead."

They kidnapped me from my family.

Then they decided they didn't want me after all and they passed me along to my grandmother – who wasn't actually my grandmother.

Then, at eleven years old, I found out my dad wasn't actually my father.

Now, at twenty I find out my mom isn't my mom. The father she said was mine when I was eleven is still not actually my father. I have no family. I am a mutt.

Eventually I found out my biological family was living in Pampa, Texas. I have a mother and brothers! I traveled up to meet them. Finally, I would be part of a family – my family.

But I was never really accepted. I was kept at a distance, alone, isolated from the rest. My marriage at this point had fallen apart. I had a son of my own, now, and had gotten remarried. My son started going to a church. And after a week-long church camp, my boy had gotten saved. He surrendered to be a missionary. That time the children's minister told him his first mission would be his father. I finally went to a service after weeks of asking. The preacher stood up and said they wanted to start a bus ministry. They needed drivers to go pick up kids who had no other way to get to church. I volunteered. I have a CDL. I'm perfect for the job. I finally felt like there was a way for me to serve, a way for me to be a part of something. The preacher disagreed.

"We would never allow someone who looks like you to drive a bus and pick up kids."

I have tattoos. I have a colorful past. I wanted to serve. I wanted to be a part of something. Once again, I was rejected.

I was working with this man, Rod, and every day he'd invited me to his church.

I was like, "No, no, I'm not going to your church." But every day he kept on asking. He wouldn't stop.

He tells me, "Alright, you ain't gotta come on a Sunday. You can come on a Wednesday. We have chicken fried steak and I will pay for your meal."

I said, "I done told you I'll be there."

So, I showed up and my kids liked it. They liked it a lot. A man named Marty was heading up their children's ministry and they liked it. I came in and just kind of sat there. I didn't really talk to anybody. Alright, I thought, we'll try it on Sunday.

I didn't like people. I didn't trust people. I didn't want anyone coming into my zone. My wife, Tabitha, said I was cruel. I just didn't want anyone to bother me. My first Sunday visiting this church, a guy named Rick came up to me. He was all shaking my hand, hugging me, telling me he loved me...man, I don't know you!

But it worked. I came in. I was accepted. They even let me serve. Over the years I have worked with kids in the children's ministry, I have driven buses and vans to pick up kids and bring them to church, I have gone to Port Arthur on mission trips, and I've helped with the media ministry. My favorite ministry, my number one, is the baptistery. I love the baptistery. You get to see people who are broken and at their lowest moment, maybe even feeling ashamed of who they are, and they go in to get baptized and they come out ready to go – ready to start something new. I get to pray with them before they get baptized. We pray every single time, and I love it.

I love this man. He has helped countless people who have come forward to be baptized in our church home. His passion to see these people, who were once broken, find healing is amazing. He may have felt like a mutt. He may have felt unloved. But now he is a part of a family that is larger than this world. When he felt isolated, alone, and unclean, God came and healed him. Now suddenly he is the-man-who-used-to-be-a-mutt and now has a family who loves him.

He's no longer a mutt. He is a child of the Living God.

I have sat with him, served with him, and I have watched him point people to Jesus. When he was alone, when he was stolen from his family, when he was rejected, when he was at his lowest, God saw him and said, "Mutt, I love you! I will rescue you! I will redeem you!"

His testimony that was once one of isolation and rejection, of pain and of dejection, is now one of healing and redemption. God took him and made him whole! It's the same story with Simon the Leper. When he was alone and rejected, when he was unclean and ostracized, God found him. God healed him and made him clean.

You may feel lonely and dejected. You may have a past that is crazier than anything I can imagine. I want you to know that my Jesus got up on the cross and died to pay the price for the sins of all mankind. He came to love you and give you the chance for eternal life – a new life with Him. He came so that you can walk with Him in victory! You can stand up and you don't have to yell, "I'M UNCLEAN! I'M UNCLEAN!" You can yell, "I'M SAVED! I'M SAVED! BY THE BLOOD OF JESUS, I AM SAVED!"

Some people don't have testimonies like this. Some people might say, "I was raised in the church and I didn't have anything crazy like this happen to me." But there are others in the church who have been there and what they need is someone to put an arm around them and love them. They need us to love them and not make them feel ashamed for the life they used to live and the scars on their bodies from past mistakes. Tell them they are something of value in the eyes of Jesus Christ. There are people in the church who are broken, hurting, and lonely. What we need to do is love one another. We needed to point them to Jesus Christ.

Praise God for the trials in our lives that bring us to Christ. Praise God that you no longer have to be a mutt – you can be a child of the Living God!

RAHAB THE PROSTITUTE...

For a while I was under spiritual attack. Our church would be going through a period of growth and I had received comments about how it's too much and there were too many new faces. Or I would see a picture floating around social media with a picture of a church packed full of people alongside an image of a small congregation with the caption "when the truth is preached nobody comes." I would stare at this picture and become more and more concerned. My church was growing. Was I not preaching the truth? I allowed these kinds of things to give Satan a foothold in my life. It became a source of contention for me.

As I battled with this, I came to the realization that I, fully believing in spiritual warfare, had been fighting with some very real demons. I know that Satan is out to steal, kill, and destroy. I also know that he is a toothless lion because my Jesus got up on the cross and ripped out Satan's teeth. He no longer has any power over Christians, and he has no power over me unless I allow it.

I have been so weighed down with so much and worried about my sermons along with the growth in my church.

People keep saying that no one wants to hear the truth, yet my church is growing. I know I am preaching the truth every Sunday. Every week I talk about Jesus and what He did for us – and still my congregation grows. I think there is actually a great desire for the truth. People hunger to know where they stand with the living God! I honestly believe that.

But at the same time, I know that we are living in a wicked generation. We are so caught up fighting against the progression of the acceptance of homosexuality in our world while Christians within the church are choosing to live together outside of marriage. We don't talk about that though. We don't talk about the sexual landscape of the world and how it has grabbed a hold of us. We want to point out that sin that is disgusting to us and ignore all of the others – but all sin is repulsive to the Lord. The truth is we need to stand on the word of God.

Sexual sin has a hold of a lot of us. According to a 2017 global study by ***Norton by Symantec***, one in six people admit to using public Wi-fi to watch adult content. This isn't private internet searches, this is public wi-fi searches for pornography. Hotels, restaurants, work, bus stations, etc... This is how rampant pornography has become. I cannot say that I'm completely immune to lust. It is a struggle I have to deal with. I come from a past where sexual sins absolutely had a hold of me. It is everywhere. It can grab people and dig its claws into them before they even realize it. It can destroy marriages and break people.

In the second chapter of Joshua, two spies from the Israelite army who sneak into Jericho. They end up at a woman's house where they hid from soldiers who had been sent to capture them. This woman is called "Rahab the Prostitute." She covered for the two Israelites by sending the soldiers the wrong way while the spies hid on her roof.

We see Rahab (the prostitute) only five times in Scripture. We see her in Joshua 2 and 6. We see her again later in the genealogy of Jesus Christ in Matthew. We see her in the second chapter of James, and again in chapter 11. Of the five times we see her, only once is she called by her name. Four out of the five times she is called "Rahab the Prostitute." Even beyond what she did and how she helped save the Israelites she is still labeled Rahab the Prostitute.

Why? We know that she had a moment when she was talking to the spies and admitted that she knew who they were. She admitted to the fear her people felt about the Israelites and their God. She even proclaimed their God as the true God above all gods! Her own legacy, the lineage of Jesus Christ, still does not cleanse her of this moniker – Rahab the Prostitute.

I believe that she repented. I think that she gave up her life of prostitution after the fear of the Lord came upon her. I believe she didn't want to walk in that life anymore, but because that's who she was – because it's how she was identified – she could not escape the label that she had been given.

There are some sexual sins that hold onto people so strongly, even to the point of becoming their identity, that it's like they can't escape who they once were.

We don't know her past. I doubt she woke up one day and said to herself, "You know what? I think I'll go sell my body for money." I don't think that is what happened. I believe that sexual immorality grabbed ahold of her and that people started offering to pay her for sex. She remained in that lifestyle until it became who she was – Rahab the Prostitute. I am not saying that everyone who is in sexual relationships outside of marriage are prostitutes. Yet it is clear in Scripture that if you are a Christian, if you follow Christ as Lord and Savior of your life, and you continue on in that sinful relationship without correcting it, you have then prostituted yourself.

That is a bold statement, and definitely not a popular one to make, but it is a Scriptural one.

But anyone joined to the Lord is one spirit with Him. Run from sexual immorality! "Every sin a person can commit is outside the body." On the contrary, the person who is sexually immoral sins against his own body. Don't you know that your body is a sanctuary of the Holy Spirit who is in you, whom you have from God? You are not your own, for you were bought at a price. Therefore, glorify God in your body.

1 Corinthians 6:17-20 HCSB

Imagine it this way, on his wedding day a groom is standing at the altar waiting for his bride. She comes walking down the aisle dressed in white. Excitedly, he watches her move toward him, pure and spotless. His bride! The Lord tells us that we, the church, are the bride of Christ! Here comes Jesus, standing in front of us with his hands outstretched waiting for His bride. The doors open wide and the church walks in but with all of the things we hold onto, all of the sins we refuse to let go of, can we honestly wear that white dress?

The way we speak, could we really wear the dress of a pure spotless bride? The things we search on the internet when nobody is around, could we still wear that dress? The thoughts in our heads when we see things that tempt us, could we be the pure spotless bride?

I look at Rahab and remember that even when we get to "The heroes of faith," in Hebrews, Abraham is not listed as "The man who says his wife is his sister." Moses is not "Moses who struck the rock." Noah is not "the man who got drunk." Only one person carries a moniker here: Rahab the Prostitute. She had to overcome it!

Promiscuity is all around us. It's getting a hold of the Church. It's getting a hold of Christians individually. It has gotten to the point where we have started accepting different sins as being "okay." It's "okay" to live together outside of marriage. It's "okay" to have sexual relationships outside of the confines of marriage. Sexual promiscuity is "okay." But it is not. It is not "okay." How arrogant of us to say "God, bless us," and "How dare there not be prayer in schools," and "God bless America," when we are allowing sexual promiscuity to run rampant? How can we ask God to bless our country when we allow 54 million abortions to happen?

For everything that belongs to the world – the lust of the flesh, the lust of the eyes, and the pride in one's lifestyle – is not from the Father, but is from the world.
1 John 2:16 HCSB

You don't have to travel very far from home in the world today before you will be bombarded by temptation. Satan does that to us! He throws it in our face. I frequently drive to a nearby city to visit my wife's family, and every time I enter the city limits one of the first things I see is a giant billboard with an advertisement for a popular restaurant plastered on its face. Whether I want to see it or not, it is always there – a large sign covered with the cleavage of a woman that somehow is supposed to be an advertisement for food. My kids have even noticed it and have asked me about the sign.

Sexual imagery is everywhere. I have seen it in ads and I have seen it on television. I was watching a show with some of my friends and two of the characters started having sexual relations outside of marriage. I was disturbed. Sexual temptations are something I struggle with in my life and here it is on a television show that I am watching with my friends. Am I the only one feeling convicted about this? Christians have been largely silent on the subject.

Here is what Satan has done:

Have you ever looked at angels in the Bible? They are terrifying creatures. When people in the Bible encounter angels, they fall to their faces in fear. Angels always appear in the form of a powerful man or even in the form of a scary, fearsome creature. Yet here is what Satan did. He took the cute, chubby little babies from mythology and infantilized these awesome angels of God. He took these mighty warriors and devalued, demeaned, and deflated them. WE stick these pretty, soft angels on the tops of our Christmas trees without even realizing what Satan has done. He has taken creatures with awesome, terrifying power and he has weakened their image.

Even the word awesome has been weakened. I'm just as guilty as anyone in this. I say it all the time. My wife will ask me what I'm doing, and I usually answer, "I'm eating tacos" (because that's usually what I'm doing). She will ask me how they are and I will say "Oh, they are awesome!" When really the meaning of the word is so much more than that. Awesome: so powerful that it fills you with awe. Awesome is a word that describes being inspired to the point of a reverential fear. Hearing it defined that way changes how we want to use it, does it not? Who should we describe as awesome? Who has awesome power? God does. God is awesome.

Satan has watered it down from a definition of our God's omnipotence to how we describe great tacos. Satan has also done this with sexual relations. We are not disturbed by sexual sins anymore because we have been in a spiritual battle over it, and we do not even realize it is happening. He already has a hold on our thinking and has twisted it until we've been tricked into believing that sexual immorality doesn't matter.

The Barna Group, along with Josh McDowell Ministry, did a study called "The Porn Phenomenon: The Explosive Growth of Pornography and How It's Impacting Your Church, Life, and Ministry." There were some eye-opening, but not totally surprising, claims found in their research. Among teens ages 13-17: 8% view porn daily; 18% weekly; 17% once or twice a month. Among those in the ages of 18-24: 12% viewed pornographic content daily; 26% weekly; 19% once or twice a month. For those in the ages of 25-30: 8% viewed adult content daily; 17% weekly; 20% once or twice a month. The problem is real! But in the same way that while the Israelites are crossing the Jordan and going to the Promised Land, God still shows His redemptive power even in the midst of it all when they show up at the house of a prostitute who rescues them and calls out to the Lord. In her unlikely house, they find safety, and she finds God and redemption. She finds redemption that leads her from a house of ill repute all the way to the lineage of Christ.

She finds redemption that puts her in standing with the Heroes of Faith, and even further to the testimony of what God can do in all our lives. Even in that place, they find the story of God's forgiveness.

We see redemption over and over again in Scripture. We see it with the woman who is dragged to the feet of Jesus with men standing around her ready to stone her to death. (Which, by the way, has it ever struck you as odd that they say she was caught in the act of adultery but where is the man?) Then, as Jesus is drawing on the ground and they are trying to get Him to condemn this woman's actions, He simply says that if any of them have never sinned then that person can throw the first stone. She looks at Jesus and He asks her if no one condemns her. She says "no" and He replies, "then neither do I." A lot of people use this Scripture to excuse a sinful lifestyle, but they forget the last part of what He tells her. He tells her to "go and sin no more."

Walk away from the things you are holding onto. Do not live that life anymore. We see it in the Bible many times. We see it with David and Bathsheba. David, who is described as a man after God's own heart, is looking at Bathsheba with lust. People try to say "she was bathing out there on purpose! She wanted him to see her and be tempted!" That's not the point though. David looked at her and he gave into temptation. He did anything in his power to make her his. He even went so far as to have her husband murdered so he could have her. Yet even from sinful roots of affairs and murder, God redeemed their relationship and they produced a son who became the king who built the temple for God.

One of my favorite stories of sexual redemption in the Bible is the story of Hosea. It is such a powerful story. Hosea is trying to seek the Lord as he lives his life when suddenly God says to him "Hosea, Israel has turned from me." They're a wicked and adulterous generation – but I love them. Here is what I want to do as an illustration of Israel. I want you to marry a promiscuous woman." She is promiscuous, lusting after and sleeping with other men and Hosea knows this and he loves her anyway! They have children together, but her heart is unrepentant.

She leaves Hosea and goes back to her lifestyle of sleeping with other men. Hosea goes looking for her. Can you imagine what that was like for him? He would have had to ask everyone he saw if they had seen his wife. Some of those men probably did not want to admit that they knew because they might have had her hidden in some back room in the shadows. He looks for her without giving up on her. Her own children call her out and ask her to repent and she won't. Anyone, man or woman, who has an unrepentant heart will find themselves falling back into their old lifestyles and sinful habits.

God tells Hosea that this is what Israel had done to Him. They had prostituted themselves out to other gods. They had left Him. But He is going to redeem them!

I will heal their apostasy; I will freely love them,
for My anger will have turned from him.
Hosea 14:4 HCSB

Years down the road Hosea looks and sees this old, washed up prostitute who is for sale on the auction block. He looks at her and recognizing her, he yells out, "That's my bride and I love her!" He goes and buys her back. He buys back the woman who left him, who left their children, who ran off to sleep with other men. He buys her back. He takes one look at her and declares that she is his and he loves her. He *redeems* her.

God tells us that He is going to do the same thing. He looks at a lustful generation, slaves to our sin, being sold on the auction block, and He still sends His son to pay the price to redeem us. Just as Hosea paid for Gomer at the auction, Christ got up on the cross to pay the price for all of mankind's sins. He saw us in our adulterous state, and He still cried out, "That's my bride! She is mine and I love her!"

There is another story in the Bible about a woman receiving sexual redemption. There is the story about the woman who goes out to the well to fetch water. She goes out alone at a time when the other women are certain to not be there. Why? Because she is sleeping with the other women's husbands. She goes to the well, and Jesus is there. He asks her to get Him a drink of water. Through her shock, she asks Him how He, a Jewish man, could be asking her for water. He tells her that if she only knew who she was talking to that all she would have to do is ask, and He could give her "living water." Immediately she perks up. Where can she get this living water so she doesn't have to keep making this shameful trip to the well every day? Every day she must walk out with her jar, during the hottest part of the day, past all of these people who look at her and whisper about who she is and what she has done. Shame covers her. Her sinful past clings to her. She hears about this living water, and she gets excited. "Give me the living water so I never have to go to the well again!"

Jesus tells her who He is. She comes to the realization that she is talking to the Messiah and she runs back into town. She stands in front of the entire town and shouts that she has met a man who told her everything she had ever done. She had met the Messiah!

Imagine there is a prostitution ring in your town or in your neighborhood and one day a prostitute, after having come to know Jesus Christ as her savior, is so overwhelmed and filled with joy that she bursts through the doors of the church and runs straight down the middle aisle. Imagine people in the pews watching, some of them may have even been customers of hers at one time, yet undaunted she runs through the center of the sanctuary straight to the front and yells, "Come see a man who told me everything I ever did and showed me forgiveness!"

Can you imagine that shutting your church down? The Scripture gives us the idea that everyone in the village heard her and followed her out to see who she was talking about. It even says that half the people believed in Jesus based on what she said and the other half believed based on His testimony. Did you catch that? Half of the people in her village came to know Jesus Christ as Messiah and Savior based purely on her testimony!

No matter where you are in your battle against sexual lust in your life and no matter how it has its grip on you, Jesus got up on the cross and said, "You are mine! I am buying you back! I am redeeming you!" You can stand up and say to the world, "Look! Here is a man who told me everything I have ever done and yet still loved me and forgave me!" A forgiveness so great that even a prostitute trapped in one of the worst types of sexual addiction, can stand up, be redeemed, and even be counted as a hero of faith.

My Jesus loves you. But listen to me, Bride of Christ. It is time to repent and run to Him. I have counseled men who have found themselves in adulterous relationships through social media. I have counseled women who have stepped out of their marriages because of lust in their hearts. No congregation of believers is immune. No town is exempt. It will not be long before the Son of Man returns, and we need to stand before Him and obey His words, "Go and sin no more."

We need to repent. We use that word frequently, but do we really understand what it means? It is the idea of someone on a camel going one direction and they stop, turn around, and run back the other way. It is them turning from the way they were headed and going the complete opposite direction. We need to see people turn from the way they are going, run to Jesus, and fall on their faces at His feet. He paid the price for you. He redeemed you. Now it is up to you whether you walk with Him.

Repentance is not just saying that you will no longer be in conversations with people who you find yourself tempted by. It is also not watching shows and movies that glorify things that are evil and wicked. I am guilty of it too. I love football, but this last year I only watched one football game. I am a Miami Dolphins fan, but I could not watch them this year. Why? Truthfully, it is because it is hard for me to watch the commercials that sell sex each week. I struggle with it.

We need to repent and turn to Jesus Christ! If Rahab the prostitute can stand up, repent, and be redeemed, and held up as a hero of faith, then we can do the same. We can stand up and repent. We can be forgiven.

It does not matter what monikers you carry. It does not matter what shame you carry around on your shoulders. Your past does not change the fact that Jesus paid the price to redeem you. My own mother stood up at our church home and gave her testimony that she had two abortions before me and had planned to abort me as well. She stands up now as someone who has been redeemed by the blood of Jesus Christ. God can do the same for you. You too can be redeemed.

MATTHEW THE TAX COLLECTOR...

There are many times in life when we feel abandoned or alone. My grandfather, my father, and my cousin, who was also my best friend, all committed suicide. There have been many times throughout my life when people have walked away from me. I went through child custody cases when I was a kid, and I remember feeling alone frequently.

There are times in our lives when you might feel like you are absolutely by yourself. There are times when you are lonely because of other people's actions, but there are also times when you are lonely because of your own actions. I have been alone because of things I did to alienate people and push them away. Despite that, there were times when, even though I felt completely alone, God made Himself known to me. I knew that I was not truly alone then.

Everybody, at some point, has felt moments of loneliness. They have felt utterly alone, like nobody cared or was watching over them. I have felt that way and am confident you have too. Whether it was the result of your own choices or other situations in your life, I believe we can all identify with having been broken at some point in our lives.

As Jesus went on from there, He saw a man named Matthew sitting at the tax office, and He said to him, "Follow Me!" So, he got up and followed Him.

Matthew 9:9 HCSB

When the book of Matthew was written, tax collectors were usually ostracized and alienated from the rest of society. They were looked down upon by others. The Roman government had come in and taken over Israel. Rome had taken over many nations at this point, and for the government to function, and roads to be built, they issued taxes. It is not that different from today when our government uses taxes to fund programs and build and repair roads. It even affects our views of politicians. Our support may hinge on their opinions on taxation. One of the main reasons tax collectors were hated so openly is because they could overtax the people so that they could pay Rome but keep a cut of the money for themselves. In fact, tax collectors were so disliked that Jesus even used them to rebuke people who are continuously living in sinful lifestyle.

If he pays no attention to them, tell the church. But if he doesn't pay attention even to the church, let him be like an unbeliever and a tax collector to you.

Matthew 18:17 HCSB

Jesus did not say, "Let him be like a Pharisee or a scribe to you." He did not say, "Let them be like those who persecute Me!" No. When describing how to respond to someone who completely and continuously rejected the Word of God, Jesus said to let them be like a tax collector to you. When someone within the church continues to live in habitual sin – even after having been approached privately, after discussing it with them and with witnesses, and after you have stood before the church and publicly confronted them about their sin – you are instructed to treat them like a tax collector. Treat them like tax collectors who sold out their own people, their own families, just so they could make a profit.

They were so despised, rabbis would tell the Israelites to not even socialize with them. They could not even make atonement sacrifices because they were not allowed to enter synagogues or temples. They were completely isolated from the rest of their community. You could not practice religious beliefs with them, you could not associate with them, and if you had a family member who became a tax collector, you had to make a choice: you could choose them, or you could walk away from them and choose to follow the Lord. There was no in between. Tax collectors were completely shunned.

One day Jesus walked by and He saw a man named Matthew sitting at a table outside of the port area where ships would dock, affording him the opportunity to collect large taxes. Jesus sees him sitting there, looks right at him as if into his very soul, and He says to him, "Follow me." Just those two words! "Follow me." That simple phrase rocked Matthew to the core. It broke him down to the very essence of who he was. The rawness of his life, all the pain of being rejected and shunned, boiled up to this moment where because of Matthew's decisions, everyone else had turned their back on him. Everyone but Jesus.

I love that statement. "...but Jesus."

But Jesus sees him. He looks at Matthew and says, "Follow me." I can just see Matthew in this moment breaking down and crying. Matthew, who is completely isolated from his friends and family, sees Jesus – a good Jewish man whose reputation is quickly growing as His ministry spreads. This same Jesus looks at him and despite who Matthew is says, "Follow me." Matthew stands up, leaves his table and bags of money and his parchments of carefully calculated figures, and runs to follow Jesus.

Something about that moment broke Matthew's heart. Something about Jesus' eyes or His tone of voice when He said "follow me" broke through years of heartache and tore down walls and barriers, reaching Matthew right where he was.

When I was nine years old I went to a boys' camp. The man who invited me to it lived across the street from me. He ran a Royal Ambassadors program at First Baptist in Dumas, Texas. Years later when he was visiting me at a church I pastored, I asked him why he had invited me to that camp.

He said, "Dallas, I figured if there was ever a kid who was going to hell it was you."

Oh thanks! What a wonderful answer!

Then again, to illustrate his point, I got in trouble for throwing gourds at the other kids' heads. They brought me in three separate times for pegging these kids with gourds. After calling my dad, along with trying everything else they could think of to stop me, I hit one of the adults with a gourd. At that point, my neighbor paddled me in front of the entire camp. After having tried everything they could, I was still so unruly it took something drastic to change my behavior.

That night, my neighbor came to me and said, "Dallas, I had a dream. You were kneeling and there was a dark shadow and a white light in front of you. As you knelt I heard a voice ask, 'Which way will you go?' I don't know what that means, but I felt like I needed to tell you." He walked back to his bunk to go to bed, leaving me to my thoughts. I will be honest with you – it freaked me out!

A little while after that, another counselor came up to me and told me he had a dream. He said, "You were kneeling down with a sword in front of you. There was a white light and a dark shadow, and I heard someone say, 'Dallas, which way will you go?' I don't know what it means but I needed to tell you about it." I remember thinking, "Man! What goes on at these RA camps? This is crazy!"

I will never forget what happened the next day. I was sitting there, and they started preaching about salvation. Somewhere along the way they brought up grace and forgiveness. I remember hearing that and realizing that my sins could be forgiven. I realized that even my mom and dad with all their struggles and their sins could be forgiven. I knew then that I did not have to walk down the same paths that they had. Their struggles did not have to become my struggles. I was only nine years old and I should not have had the problems that I had. I was so bitter, and angry, and hurt. I can remember the speaker walking by me and talking about grace and forgiveness. God could give me that forgiveness! It was as if I could hear Jesus, just like Matthew had, saying "Follow me." I stood up and I chose to follow.

My life has not been perfect by any means. There have been hurts, pains, and bumps in the road, but He has always been there with me. He has never given up on me. He called me to follow Him and I did. He loves me!

Luke sheds a little more light on the story of Matthew. In his gospel he calls Matthew "Levi". At this time, it was not an uncommon practice in the Jewish faith for men their age to have two different names. Matthew chose to identify himself in the Gospel with a very common, low profile name. Luke however, calls him Levi.

Levi is a name that has history. It is an important, respectable name. It came from the Levitical priesthood. His family gave him this name and it could have been because it is such a respectable name, or it may have been because he had a religious background, or it could even have been that he came from the line of Levitical priests. I don't know why – but what I do know is that the name held respectability, and for whatever reason Matthew chose not to identify himself by it. Maybe he felt like he had fallen too far and did not deserve the name. Maybe he felt like Matthew was a more appropriate name for a tax collector. Maybe he felt like someone so ostracized from the rest of his people did not deserve a name like Levi. But Luke calls him by his name. It is almost as if Luke is saying, "Matthew won't tell you everything, but I will!"

After this, Jesus went out and saw a tax collector named Levi sitting at the tax office, and He said to him, "Follow Me!" So, leaving everything behind, he got up and began to follow Him.
Luke 5:27-28 HCSB

Here is where Matthew describes this as a bunch of men reclining at a dinner table. Luke gives us a clearer picture.

Then Levi hosted a grand banquet for Him at his house. Now there was a large crowd of tax collectors and others who were guests with them. But the Pharisees and their scribes were complaining to His disciples, "Why do you eat and drink with tax collectors and sinners?"

Jesus replied to them, "The healthy don't need a doctor, but the sick do. I have not come to call the righteous, but sinners to repentance."
Luke 5:29-32 HCSB

What is so ironic about this is it was the religious leaders who chose not to talk to them. It was the Pharisees and the educated men who shunned those sinners and questioned Jesus' association with them. They did not talk about repentance, forgiveness, or grace. When Luke calls their dinner a grand banquet, it is as if he is saying that while Matthew described it as just a little affair, it was more likely that Matthew used everything he had to create this dinner and invited all of his friends. He did not invite just the well-to-do either. He invited the people who were around him. He invited the tax collectors and the sinners. He invited those who had been cast out. Imagine a grand banquet with a table full of tax collectors, sinners, prostitutes, and the outcasts all who have been rejected by society – and reclining at the table with them was Jesus.

And they start having church.

Isn't that what church is? Isn't church when we invite Jesus in and He comes into our midst and we fellowship with Him? Isn't it when we follow Him? Isn't that where church comes from? That is what was happening with Matthew. He invited Jesus in and was fellowshipping with Him. The religious leaders who had been leading the way for years and years, were unhappy with Jesus because He was changing everything up. The synagogues were changing. People had started following this radical named Jesus, who was wreaking havoc in the land. They were following Him and scrutinizing everything He did.

These religious aficionados show up at Matthew's dinner party – but why are they there? Why did they show up? I bet it was because they heard about what Jesus was doing. I'm sure one of them said to the others, "Hey! You won't believe what's going on at Matthew the Tax Collector's house! He is throwing a huge party, and he invited Jesus!" They went to mock Matthew and Jesus. They show up at the party to ridicule Jesus asking, "How dare He eat with sinners?"

Praise God that Jesus shows up for sinners! Praise God that Jesus showed up for a sinner like me when I was nine years old. Praise God that He met with you as a sinner.

Yet the Pharisees, with their superior attitudes, wondered, "Why would He eat with sinners? Why would He eat with those kinds of people?" Jesus comes back at them with His response, and I think about it often.

Have you ever noticed that sometimes when Jesus answered questions, He would do so sarcastically? I don't know where people got this idea that He is this hippie Jesus and "everything is cool, man." That is not a complete picture of Him. The man made whips out of cords and drove thieves out of His temple. He meant business. Sometimes when people tell me that my sermon "stepped on their toes", I just want to say "Hey, I could have made whips out of cords!"

Jesus looks at the Pharisees as they are mocking Him for eating with sinners and His response is almost like, "Oh, I get why you're confused. I didn't come to heal the healed. I came to heal the sick. You righteous must not need me." Self-righteous religious people are still driving people away from Christ. They are still mocking others. They are still knocking people down and laughing at them. We get this idea that if we are so holy in our religious practice then we are better than everyone else. This idea that if someone gets saved and they come into a church wearing shorts (God forbid!) or if you don't wear a suit and tie to church, you must be terrible people.

If you have a suit and tie and want to wear them to church, that is great. If all you have are hand-me-down clothes and flip-flops, then that is great, too. Wear what you have. Quit making church what it isn't. It is about coming together to talk to the One who can set us free. It is about meeting the One who says, "Follow me," and you get up, leave your sinful lifestyle, and follow Him. That is what Christianity is about. It is leaving who you were and following Him. It is dying to your old life to follow Christ.

Then Jesus told his disciples, "If anyone wants to come with Me, he must deny himself, take up his cross, and follow Me.

Matthew 16:24 HCSB

Church is a group of sinners gathering together and having a grand banquet for the One who can set them free.

It does not matter how righteous you are. It does not matter how many verses you have memorized or how many countries you have been to. It certainly does not matter how sharp you look. Your religiosity does not impress Jesus. What does is the heart of a sinner saying, "I will get up, and I will follow You."

Repeatedly in Scripture we see stories of tax collectors. The story of the infamous Zacchaeus who was so corrupt he tried to make amends for everything he had done. We see the story of the Pharisee and the publican in Luke 18. Why does Jesus keep drawing attention to tax collectors repenting? Very rarely does Jesus talk about Pharisees turning to follow Christ. Over and over again Jesus points to the lowest of the low and shows them turning and following Christ.

When we lived in a small town in the Texas Panhandle, we bought a house and moved our family into it. At one point it needed some work done, so we hired a contractor and got to work. There was an electrician who was working on some wiring and every time he came to our house I would try to talk with him about the Gospel. He would have none of it. He would find any excuse at the drop of a hat to get out of hearing me talk about God. He was so good at getting out of our conversations that even though he was working on my house three weeks longer than planned, I still had trouble getting him to hear anything about God. It started to become a challenge to me. I began thinking one day this guy and I are going to sit down and get this all out. I was determined that I was going to tell him about Jesus, but he was so good at dodging me.

One day I went to the house, and he was in the bathroom working on the lights. He mentioned them being difficult and that they would take more time which I know means more money. So, he starts to explain that the attic space is only big enough for one man to shimmy into and work on and his buddy was up there already working on the wiring.

I said, "So your buddy is already in there?"

"Yeah, he is, and I can't get in there so it's going to take a long time."

There it is. There's my in. So, I said to him that it was a perfect time for us to finally have a chance to sit down and talk. His eyes were huge as he realized he had been caught. He was always nice and polite to me, he just did not want to talk about Jesus. We went downstairs, and I started sharing with Ricky, the electrician, about Jesus. I went through the same process I do with everyone I share with. I walked him through what is called the "good person test." I asked him if he had ever lied. He admitted that he had, and that he was a sinner because that is what he expected that I wanted to hear. So I asked him to get more specific.

I asked, "If you tell a lie, what are you?"

"I'm a liar."

So, I asked him if he'd ever robbed anything before adding, "Now Ricky, you just admitted you're a liar so try to be honest with me."

He laughed and told me a few stories of transgressions past. I told him about how Jesus said if you have ever lusted in your heart, you are guilty of adultery. I asked him if he had ever lusted in his heart. I asked him if he had ever had hatred in his heart and explained that in the book of Matthew, Jesus teaches us that if we have hatred in our heart toward someone, we are guilty of murder. One by one we worked our way through all of these and finally I told him:

"Ricky, one day you're going to stand in front of God and He's going to say, 'Why should I let you into Heaven?' What are you going to say?"

"I don't know. Maybe that I'm a good person."

"Ricky, you can't be a good enough person. You could steal my car and feed the homeless out of it for thirty years, but if one day you are brought before a judge, he's not going to care what you did with the car for thirty years! All he cares about is the fact that you stole the car. You are going to stand before the Good Judge one day. Why would He let you into Heaven?"

"I don't know."

I began to tell Ricky why God would let him in. I told him about how God loved us all so much that He sent His Son to die for him. I told him how Jesus took every one of his sins upon Himself. I told him that Jesus took every lustful thought, every lie, every hateful thought or action, to the cross. I told him that Jesus took everything to the cross to pay the price for him. Then I told him that Jesus gave His life so that His perfect blood could wash Ricky clean.

On the floor in my basement Ricky gave his life to Jesus. I got him a Bible the next day. He called me and told me he wanted to surprise his family. His goal was to get his whole family to church and surprise them by getting baptized. He told his family that I had been inviting him to church and he wanted them all to go just because he was curious about it. He was trying to get them all to come on the same day but couldn't seem to get the schedule worked out with everyone. So, he told no one he was a Christian yet. One day about a month later he calls me up and says, "Dallas, I think God has big plans for me. Do you think He does?" I remember saying, "Ricky, I know God has big plans for you, brother. I know He does."

Two weeks after that phone call Ricky died of a sudden heart attack. His body was weakened from all the drugs he had used over the years. Even though he no longer used, his body could not handle any more trauma. When I went to his house I could immediately see how much his family was struggling. They weren't just grieving over his death.

They were grieving his soul. They just knew he had died and gone to Hell.

"I remember telling them, "NO! No, Ricky gave his life to Jesus!"

They didn't believe me.

"He really did! I can show you."

I went and got his Bible and showed them the day he had given his life to Christ. I told them how he had planned to surprise them with his baptism. They finally believed me, and I told them about the phone call when Ricky asked me about God's plan for him. I asked them if they believed that Ricky and I were right about the plans. They said they did. So, I asked if I could officiate his funeral. I told them that I felt like Ricky's funeral had the ability to bring in people that would never set foot in a church otherwise.

It was as if Ricky's funeral became a banquet feast where he invited all his friends to come celebrate his life. His one desire was that Jesus be the center of the banquet. As the funeral went on, I shared the story of Ricky's life and how he had given his life to Christ in my basement. I then shared how others could give their lives to Christ too. There in that small chapel, filled with men and women who did not look like your stereotypical churchgoers, we had church. Fourteen people gave their lives to Christ on that day.

That is what happens when people get together and celebrate Jesus Christ and what he did for us. That is what happens when we invite Him to our "grand banquets" and invite people in. I do not want a church that is so holy and righteous that we make the rest of the world feel unwelcome. I want us to always remember that we too were dead in our trespasses but are now alive in Jesus Christ. I want to see people completely leave their sinful ways and follow Jesus. I want you to remember that you have influence with people that other Christians will never have. The church was not meant to be a place were sick people go to be healed. You are the church. Hold a "grand banquet" and invite your friends to it. Ask Jesus to be the center of it. The church building is just a place where we all gather together. The church is you. Show your friends who Jesus is and watch what He will do.

YOU DECIDE…

Jesus Christ is the soon-returning king. Are you ready? If right at this moment, wherever you are, as you are reading this paragraph, you heard a trumpet blast in the sky – would you be ready? Would you be ready to stand before the living God? I personally believe that 98% of all biblical prophecy has been fulfilled. This is the truth. The reality of it is 2% of prophecies remain to be fulfilled. He is coming back!

I have written about several people from the Bible who are known by a specific moniker stemming from a sordid past. It all started with Saul in the book of Acts. He was saved after seeing Jesus on the road to Damascus. Afterward he began his travels as Paul the Apostle, where he began preaching and teaching about Jesus. Everywhere he went; however, he was recognized because of his past. "Paul? Isn't that the man who…?" They would list off all the things he had done, all the persecutions and atrocities he had committed – and rightly so. He *was* the man who did those things.

We looked at others who, like Paul, were known by their past conditions or actions. We read about Simon the Leper.

How could someone so unclean be with Jesus? Rahab the Prostitute. Matthew the Tax Collector. We looked at each of these heroes of the Bible and asked, "Isn't that the one who…?" Now I want us to look at that question one more time but this time you decide who.

Jesus, while walking on this earth amongst us, posed this question to His disciples:

Who do people say that the Son of Man is? And they said, "Some say John the Baptist; others, Elijah; still others, Jeremiah or one of the prophets."
Matthew 16:13b-14 HCSB

The idea was this: we know that John the Baptist was popular. He was traveling all over, drawing huge crowds as he paved the way for the Messiah. Rumors had already begun to be spread. Is this man John the Baptist? Others thought that He might be Elijah. There was a prophecy of Elijah, alongside another prophet, returning and that when he does, he will stand at the end of times proclaiming the Messiah. Could this Jesus be Elijah returning? Could He be a resurrected Jeremiah or another one of the prophets? These were a few of the ideas of who Jesus was. It was as Jesus was casting a demon out of a mute man that a crowd of people had another idea of who Jesus might be.

Now He was driving out a demon that was mute. When the demon came out, the man who had been mute, spoke, and the crowds were amazed. But some of them said, "He drives out demons by Beelzebul, the ruler of the demons!" And others as a test were demanding of Him a sign from heaven.

Knowing their thoughts, He told them: "Every kingdom divided against itself is headed for destruction, and a house divided against itself falls. If Satan also is divided against himself, how will his kingdom stand? For you say I drive out demons by Beelzebul. And if I drive out demons by Beelzebul, who is it your sons drive them out by? For this reason, they will be your judges. If I drive out demons by the finger of God, then the kingdom of God has come to you.

Luke 11:14-20 HCSB

Some people accused Jesus of being a demon possessed man driving out other demons. Others would claim He was only a great performer, as if turning water to wine or walking on water were parlor tricks. Even as He hung on the cross, dying, people asked Him to perform more "tricks". Sadly, this has not changed much even amongst religious people. They want Jesus to perform for them when it is convenient for them. They want Him to be some version of a glorified genie-in-a-bottle. "My life is so bad I will finally look to the Bible. I know! I'll just rub the Bible and hopefully Genie-Jesus will come out and answer all of my wishes."

Some said Jesus was John the Baptist. Others claimed He was Elijah, Jeremiah, a prophet, a demon, or a performer. But then Jesus asked His disciples:

"But you," He asked them, "who do you say that I am?"
Simon Peter answered, "You are the Messiah,
the Son of the living God!"
Matthew 16:15-16 HCSB

To the believers, the men who followed Him and had seen all His works, He asked, "Who do you say that I am?" Jesus is the living God! He is the embodiment of God. He was there in the beginning when God created man "in our image". (Genesis 1:26 HCSB) He is the Word who was there in the beginning "with God, and the Word was God." (John 1:1 HCSB) Jesus knows who He is. He knows the answer to His question. He knew the hearts of His disciples and what they believed. He knows all these things but He needed to get them to this point where He could ask them this question and they could answer it. And we read Peter's words, that Jesus is the Messiah. He knows who Jesus is. But even he struggles with it. Even Peter wants to know if Jesus is really the messiah. The thing is everyone struggles with who He is. Everyone battles doubt from time to time. I want to show you, however, some who do not question who He is. Some who know exactly who Jesus Christ is and the power that He has.

Then He went down to Capernaum, a town in
Galilee, and was teaching them on the Sabbath.

They were astonished at His teaching because His message had authority. In the synagogue there was a man with an unclean demonic spirit who cried out with a loud voice, "Leave us alone! What do You have to do with us, Jesus – Nazarene? Have You come to destroy us? I know who You are – The Holy One of God!"
Luke 4:31-34 HCSB

Then they sailed to the region of the Gerasenes, which is opposite Galilee. When He got out on land, a demon-possessed man from the town met Him. For a long time, he had worn no clothes and did not stay in a house but in the tombs. When he saw Jesus, he cried out, fell down before Him, and said in a loud voice, "What do You have to do with me, Jesus, You Son of the Most High God? I beg You, don't torment me!"
Luke 8:26-28 HCSB

Do you know who doesn't question the validity and deity of Jesus Christ?

Do you know who knows without a shadow of a doubt who He is?

Do you know who is absolutely certain of Jesus Christ?

Every demon who was cast out of Heaven to this earth. They know. Oh, they know.

Jesus comes into the synagogue, the very place where they were reading the Torah and worshipping God, and the demon makes himself known and says something very peculiar. He says, "Leave us alone!" Have you ever thought about that? Why would he say that? We know a third of the angels fell and were cast out of heaven. Maybe he is saying to leave all of them alone?

Maybe.

But maybe he is saying something else. It is not a huge leap of logic to assume he may have meant "leave us alone" as in he and all of the people there he had influence over. Maybe the demon was claiming dominion and was holding on tightly to the people he was controlling.

"Leave us alone!"

As if telling Jesus to leave them alone could stop Him. Jesus, who has the power and authority over everything says,

> *"Be quiet and come out of him!" And throwing him down before them, the demon came out of him without hurting him at all.*
> **Luke 4:35b HCSB**

As they are sailing across the Sea of Galilee, the winds are picking up and waves are crashing into the sides of the boat. Jesus goes below deck and lays down to take a nap. Everybody is scared to death that the boat can't handle the winds and waves. They all start panicking and rush down to Jesus to wake Him. They do not know that He can do anything. They do not yet believe. But they wake Him and ask Him how He could be sleeping when they are all about to die. He walks to the deck and speaks to the wind and the waves. Suddenly the storm quiets. They ask, "Who could this man be that He commands the storm and calms it?"

They get ashore to a land where there are two men who are so possessed that the people in the area have bound them with chains inside of caves. The two men were so powerful that they would break their chains, strip off their clothes, and run around while the people chased them. Imagine Jesus stepping onto the shore followed by all of these other men who were still awestruck at the sight of a man saving their lives by speaking to a storm, when a demon possessed man comes running down the shore and upon seeing Jesus collapses at His feet. Falling on his face before the Son of the Living God he cried out, begging Jesus to leave them alone. "Them" because there were so many demons possessing that man that when Jesus asked him for his name he said "Legion." A legion of demons possessing a man and they all know, without a shadow of a doubt, who Jesus is. They are scared to death of Jesus because they know exactly what is coming. All the people around Jesus could not figure out who He was. Was He John the Baptist? Perhaps He was some prophet or performer. But these demons did not question it for one second. They knew.

That is why demons try to grab and hold onto us so hard. They are trying to hold on and claim dominion over people. They are trying to claim us as theirs because they know their time is short. They saw Jesus in Heaven when they were cast out. They know and believe in the promise that is coming. They know they will be cast down to eternal torment, so they are holding on as tightly as they can for as long as they can. Not only do we see it in Scripture but we can see it in the lives of people around us. I see the way they fight for and grab hold of us.

For too long we have been scared to talk about the Holy Spirit. We were afraid because we did not want sensationalism. We did not want fanaticism. I have seen it. I have seen people faking the powers of the Holy Spirit. I have seen these things. But I will not deny the reality and the power of the Holy Spirit. I am not ashamed to talk about Him. We do not like talking about spiritual warfare, demons, and Satan. We do not want people to label us and be scared of us. If I could terrify you to come to Jesus Christ, then call me the boogeyman. I would scare you to death just to get you to come to Christ if I could. But I cannot. I am not going to say that spiritual warfare isn't real. I can't say that. I have seen it. It comes after me and it tries to get a hold on me. You can talk to missionaries who have traveled the world and seen demon possessions first hand. In a town I was pastoring in, a man named James had been a missionary in Africa and he told us about demon possessions that would make your skin crawl.

You do not even have to leave the USA to see it. I went on a mission trip to Alaska and saw a very real demonic activity. There was a time when I heard people yelling my name, so I went running towards them. When I got to them they were all standing in front of this lady who suddenly hissed at them and slinked back towards the apartments she had come from. I asked them what had happened, and they told me that the woman had come out of the apartments and was punching and hitting everyone in the immediate area. They told her to leave, but she wouldn't. She kept hitting them, and they finally started yelling for me – as if I would automatically know the answer to *that* situation. Over and over they told her to leave and she growled, "You have no authority over me!" The lady I was with told her, "Yes I do! I have the authority in Jesus Christ!" That is the exact moment I ran up and heard the woman hiss.

You might think, "Oh that is a world away. Those stories happen in places like Africa and the Amazon and maybe even Alaska, but they do not happen here. Those kinds of things happen in dark places far away from me." Let me tell you one more story then.

I have mentioned I pastored a church in a small town in the Panhandle of Texas. There, in that sanctuary, a lady sat down whose husband was about to get baptized. After he had been baptized she said, "I wish I could have what you have." He told her that she could have it. She just needed to trust in Jesus as her savior and repent. She told him that she couldn't because the shadow figures would not let her.

"There are two shadow figures who follow me all the time and they whisper evil and wicked things to me. They will not let me. They were so mad that I came to church today!"

When her family came to me and told me this story, I asked them to talk to her again and ask her if the shadow figures came into the church with her. They were surprised at my response. They thought I would be shocked or just not believe them. They were scared by what she was saying, but they agreed to ask her anyway.

When they asked her if the shadows had come into the church, she replied, "No! They followed me to the doors and tried to come in, but they couldn't. They stayed outside and prowled around outside of the doors."

Later, they asked me why I had them ask that particular question, and I told them how every Sunday I would come to church, very early, and pray for a hedge of protection around it. I would pray that God would keep Satan and his forces outside of the doors of this place. I don't want a demon to come in here and try to claim dominion over us. Satan does not belong in here.

Whether these stories make you uncomfortable or not does not change the fact that the Bible tells us:

Our battle is not against flesh and blood, but against the rulers, against the authorities, against the world powers of this darkness, against the spiritual forces of evil in the Heavens.

Ephesians 6:12 HCSB

There are real demons and they are really trying to hold on. They acknowledge Him. They know who Jesus Christ is.

Remember when He cast the demon out of the mute man and the crowd accused Jesus Himself of being demonic? Look at Jesus' response to them:

If I drive out demons by the finger of God, then the kingdom of God has come to you. When a strong man, fully armed, guards hesitate, his possessions are secure. But when one stronger than he attacks and overpowers him, he takes from him all his weapons he trusted in and divides up his plunder. Anyone who is not with Me is against Me, and anyone who does not gather with Me scatters.

Luke 11:20-23 HCSB

We use this passage often to justify being strong and protecting our homes. I hold onto these verses because I used to like to fight, but God got a hold of me and told me I could not pick fights like that anymore – but I can and will protect my family. We have used this verse as a justification, but look closely at this paragraph. It is saying that a strong man can protect his house, but that when one who is stronger comes into his house he can overpower him and take what is his. It is saying that Satan has claimed earth and is trying to take hold of it. But God is the stronger One who comes into Satan's "house" and overpowers him, taking back what is His. Jesus follows it by saying that anyone who is not with Him is against Him and whoever does not gather with Him scatters.

Back to the question at hand: who do *you* say that Jesus is?

There is a word in the Bible that I love: doulos. Doulos means slave or one who was bought with a price. Scripture tells us in 1 Corinthians 6:20 that we are bought with a price. We are supposed to belong to God. We are no longer our own person but totally and completely His. We also know from Scripture that if you:

Confess with your mouth that Jesus is Lord and believe in your heart that God raised him from the dead, you will be saved.

Romans 10:9 HCSB

Put these two ideas together: a slave who was bought with a great price and somebody who calls out to their Lord, who owns them. Do you want to know what our problem is? Very few of us in the church have truly surrendered to the lordship of Jesus Christ. I get people that tell me all of the time how amazed they are when the Holy Spirit moves in the church. There are people coming in with no pretenses, hearing the Word of God, and surrendering totally to Him.

They have given everything to Him and are going on to do great and mighty things because they have called Him Lord.

They have been bought with a price, surrendered, totally His, knowing that the strong-armed man is not strong enough to stop Jesus Christ. Every year at Easter we talk about when Jesus got down on the ground, bound to a log, knowing that at any moment He could call a multitude of angels to annihilate every force standing against Him. Yet He was willingly bound and brutally beaten, mocked, crowned with thorns, and burdened with a heavy cross over his shoulders that He carried down the Via Dolorosa.

They nailed Him to the cross and hanged Him there on Calvary. The whole time He hung there He struggled to life Himself up high enough to gasp air into His lungs.

All for you.

At any moment He could have called the angels and stopped it all. He did not. He lived a life perfectly sinless.

He did it all for you.

It is as if He kicked in the doors of eternity and stomped the Devil right in his mouth. Then He climbed up on the cross to pay the price for our sins. He did this as the strong man. He was not some weakling but the strongest of strong. He climbed up that hill and died on that cross for the sins of all of mankind. All to give you the option to claim his payment for the price of your sins.

All as if to ask you,

"Who do *you* say that *I am*?"

CPSIA information can be obtained
at www.ICGtesting.com
Printed in the USA
LVHW111931210119
604681LV00006B/581/P

9 781643 485348